D0160584

the gift

the gift

An original short story
by
KENNY ROGERS
&
KELLY JUNKERMANN

THOMAS NELSON PUBLISHERS
Nashville • Atlanta • London • Vancouver

Published in Nashville, Tennessee, by Thomas Nelson, Inc., Publishers, and distributed in Canada by Word Communications, Ltd., Richmond, British Columbia.

"I'll Be There" written by Kenny Rogers and Kelly Junkermann. Copyright © 1996.

"'Til the Season Comes 'Round Again" written by John Barlow Jarvis and Randy Goodrum. Copyright © 1993, used by permission of Zomba Enterprises, Inc.

ISBN O-7852-7174-0

Printed in the United States of America
2 3 4 5 6 -- 01 00 99 90 97

As she came into view at the end of the beach, he was overwhelmed by her. Even from a distance she was beautiful. He'd always loved watching her run, her long hair bouncing from side-to-side as if she were in slow motion. Beside her as always, that ugly dog of the neighbors tried to keep up. She was in every sense "poetry in motion." As she came up even with the cottage, she turned to wave and smile, but like all the times before, the picture on the screen started rolling, ruining his image of the most-perfect thing he had ever known. But today was a good day. He'd only watched it four times. He shut off the VCR and looked around the dark house that had once been so full of life. She had died forty-nine weeks and three days ago. For all intents and purposes, so had he. He couldn't help but remember what his dad had told him when he was young. "It's those who have the most, Son, who have the most to lose."

When they got married seventeen years ago, she had promised him she'd be there to take care of him when he got older, and he had made no plans beyond her. They were known as "The Thompsons." Never Russell and Kirsten, just "The Thompsons." You never saw one without the other, joined at the hip, and they both loved it that way.

Russell had never regretted his decision to give up his job, his future, and his pension to make her last four months the best four months of her life. He had been the number three man at the largest advertising agency in Chicago. They had promised him an equity position in the firm within the next three years. He had loved his job, but none of that mattered now.

Breast cancer is a woman's worst nightmare. She had no signs whatsoever. In a routine mammogram they had discovered it, but by then it was too late. They gave Kirsten four to six months. Russell hoped he would never hear those words again as long as he lived.

There were so many things she had wanted to do and so little time to do them. But in order to have something positive in their lives, they had agreed to try. Rome was wonderful. Of all the places they went, it was the best. It was charming. It was romantic. And it was the one place where they could forget the future and get lost in the past. Kirsten had joked about spending the rest of her life there. It seemed that the Italian men couldn't keep their eyes off her and she liked seeing him jealous. As incredible as that trip was, it seemed like twenty years ago. A lot had happened since then.

None of it good. He flipped off the television and headed for the door. He needed some air.

Russell Allen Thompson walked down the streets a troubled man. He bundled his coat around him as icy Lake Michigan winds swirled. The sounds of the Salvation Army ringing their street-corner bells fell on deaf ears. He passed a storefront with fifty television sets all shapes and sizes filled with the imagery of Christmas. Russell stopped and watched as smiling children caroled in the streets. Christmas . . . it had always been a special time for him. *What a shame*, he thought. For the first time in his life, he hadn't even bothered to put up a tree.

The televisions clicked to a breaking news story. Police were chasing a late-model yellow Chevrolet. Another gangland shooting had left another teenager in critical condition. The victim, Ramone Dominguez, was a former gang member. He had become a leader in cleaning up his neighborhood. Channel 6 News reporter, Anna Allison, spoke with the grieving parent. Russell hiked up his collar around his face and continued walking. He passed the

Salvation Army pot and dug into his pocket. All his money, a crumpled wad of bills and change, went into the pot. "Merry Christmas," replied the Salvation Army Santa.

"I hope so," mumbled Russell. If he couldn't enjoy this Christmas, he might as well help someone else, he thought.

He turned the corner into a biting wind and headed for a darker side of town. A couple of homeless men cowered from the wind in makeshift shelters. Across from them, a group of young street toughs eyed him suspiciously. Only a few of the street lamps were burning and most of the storefronts were boarded up. Those that were still in business had heavy bars drawn across the windows. Russell walked deeper into the darkness. The fact that he wasn't afraid in itself frightened him. This was the last place he had ever imagined being. Russell was tempting fate, hoping fate would win.

The darkness and silence were suddenly shattered. The screech of tires, police sirens, and a helicopter searchlight tore through the night. It was as if he had stepped into a battle zone. A pair of headlights raced toward him. In the harsh glare of the streetlight, Russell recognized it as the yellow Chevy from the newscast. "This is as good a way as any," Russell said to himself as he stepped off the curb and into the path of the speeding car. The driver, who less than an hour ago had shown such total disregard for human life, swerved to miss this unknown man and struck a 5,000 volt light pole instead.

It was like a Chinese New Year as the sparks lit up the night. Russell moved in slow motion to the curb. A crowd began to gather. Police cars screeched to a halt and officers raced toward the accident. A news van pulled up. The helicopter searchlight turned the night into day. From a window three stories up, a lady began to shout in broken English. "He stop them! They could have kill him!"

The reporters and police turned toward Russell. But he had slipped into the darkness and, for some reason that he didn't know, he took off running.

He weaved in and out of the dark streets. His lungs burned and he wished he were in better shape. He stopped in a dark alley. He closed his eyes and rested his head back against a cold, gray graffittied wall. He couldn't decide whether to laugh or cry. He looked up and a light snow had begun to fall.

He whispered to himself, "God help me . . . What am I

doing?" For what seemed like an eternity, but in actuality was just a couple of minutes, the sirens blared on. They seemed louder than ever before. Then once again . . . silence.

"I don't know how the police catch anyone. They make too much noise. Don't you think?"

Russell was startled by the shivering elderly black man sitting in the shadows. The man began to cough and spoke again. "It's nice not to be alone tonight."

For some strange reason, Russell agreed. They were an unlikely couple, the troubled executive and the rumpled old black man. The two men spoke of nothing and everything. The old man spoke passionately about fate, irony, and purpose. As the wind whipped around the corner, Russell could feel the pain in the man's frail old body. He took off his topcoat, wrapped it around the old man, and started out of the alley.

"Wait," Russell heard him say. "I was brought up, you don't take gifts unless you can give something back. It's not much, but it's all I got." He handed Russell an old Brownie Hawkeye camera.

Russell hadn't seen one since the '50s. "Thanks," he said. "Will you be OK?"

The old man nodded. "No matter what you are thinking now, Mr. Thompson, *where there's future . . . there's hope.*"

Russell Allen Thompson had made a new friend, and he had a camera to prove it. As he left the alley, a chill went up his spine. He hadn't remembered telling the old man his name.

Russell turned his late-model Jag into his driveway. He lived in a nice turn-of-the-century house in Highland Park, one of Chicago's finer neighborhoods. Inside, he sat down at his worn desk, covered with photos of Kirsten. He took the camera out and placed it on the desk. He leaned back in his chair with his hands clasped behind his head. He studied the camera and what it represented. Ironically he realized he had gotten his first Christmas gift.

Russell woke the next morning surprised he had slept. He fixed himself an instant coffee. Kirsten had always fixed him

real coffee every morning. After a year he should have learned how to make it himself. But that had been Kirsten's job and he didn't care if he ever drank "real" coffee again. The little things brought back the pain of her being gone.

He flipped on the television. The TV news reporter, Anna Allison, would be right back with an uplifting Christmas story, she said. *Great,* thought Russell. A commercial came on that moved so fast it made him dizzy. He wondered who on earth could have created a commercial like that. Not him.

"Last night an unusual Christmas hero walked the Chicago streets," Anna began. "It seems an unknown man stepped in front of a speeding car. Its passengers were suspects in a gangland shooting that had just been reported live on this station. We've been told by an eyewitness on the scene that the man forced the car to crash. All the suspects were apprehended by the police."

"Sounds like a real hero," her partner, Kyle Preston, said.

"There's more. It seems that the only description they have of our hero is that he is in his mid-fifties, has gray hair and beard, and was wearing a black topcoat. The police could not find the man, but they think they found his topcoat. It was wrapped around an unidentified elderly man who had died in an alley. The deceased was an African American in his late seventies. Anyone with information about either man is asked to call Captain Heard at the 27th Precinct. It seems that even as our hero fled from one good deed he performed another."

"Quite a story," Kyle chimed in. "We could use a few more like that this Christmas."

Russell stood straight up. "Died?" he said. "I could have taken him to a hospital." *Christmas hero*, he thought. How crazy was that? He had tried to become a statistic, to join the many others who found Christmas a time of quiet desperation.

Russell picked up the phone and dialed the precinct. He could help. He'd spoken to the man. He'd spent time with him. As the phone rang he realized that, while they had talked for thirty minutes, the old man had never told him one thing about himself. Not his name or anything about his family. He hung up the phone, dazed and touched by the death of his new friend. He picked up the camera. It looked older and dirtier today than it had last night. Maybe he could take it to the police for fingerprinting. As he searched for prints, he noticed four shots had been taken on the roll of film that was in the camera.

For the first time in a long time his attention turned toward something else. It was a good feeling. Perhaps he could help identify the old man and bring some peace to his family. He breathed a sigh of excitement. Russell's thoughts had turned away from his own problems.

He dropped the film off at a Thirty Minute Photo. *Thirty minutes,* he thought. Why did everything have to be faster? As he waited inside the mall, he was surrounded by the sights and sounds of Christmas. He thought of the old man in the alley. "It's good not to be alone tonight," he had said. They had been strangers, but they had not been alone. In the mall a children's choir began to sing:

> Star of wonder, Star of night,
> Star with royal beauty bright.
> Westward leading, still proceeding
> Guide us to thy perfect light.

He watched as the shoppers hurriedly went from store to store. They seemed to be on a difficult mission rather than errands of love. He thought of how he had once been part of a company that had drilled that into people's minds.

He remembered how, as a schoolboy, he would make Christmas gifts for his parents. Simple things, like a handprint ashtray. His parents would cherish them for as long as they lived. The most special gift he had given Kirsten was a plain gold heart on a simple chain. Inside on a scrap of paper he had written "I love you." She treasured it above all the other gifts he had given her. When she wore it, it had always brought Russell a simple, all-consuming joy.

He remembered how, as a boy, he couldn't wait for Christmas Day to come. He looked over to the children who had finished their carol. Their eyes were filled with the joy of the season. Russell couldn't help but notice as the children turned to leave that the smallest child was waving to his parents and didn't follow the others. Finally, the child hurried back to join the group, and Russell felt the beginning of a smile.

He checked his watch. Thirty minutes had passed, and he picked up the pictures. "Merry Christmas," the clerk said.

"Merry Christmas," Russell mumbled. He made his way back to the car and opened the package. Inside were four photographs.

He looked at the first picture. It was a photo of Russell and the old man. It wasn't possible. Nobody had been in that alley to take a picture. It had only been the two of them. With shaking hands and a rising sense of panic, he looked through the other photos, hoping to make some kind of sense out of them. All the pictures were black and white.

The second picture was also of Russell. It looked like he was on a train kneeling beside a young woman on the floor. He had no idea where it was. He had never ridden the trains in his life

The third picture was him again. He could tell by the store signs everywhere that he was in Marshall Field's. It looked like he was in the toy department, reaching for a big white bear. The only other person was a little girl, whom he had never seen, with a huge smile on her face. The store was decorated for Christmas, but it was no Christmas he had ever spent!

The fourth picture was even more puzzling. There were

no faces, but even from the back he recognized that horrible cowlick in the back of his hair. He was standing at the side of what looked like a hospital bed. He shivered, but not from the cold.

Something strange was going on. First an old man in an alley had known his name without being told. Now he was looking at pictures of himself in situations and places he had never been. Russell Thompson was scared. Religion means different things to different people. Russell and Kirsten had never been religious, but there had always been a spiritual side to them. What was happening to him now was way out of his league. He needed help. He had to talk to someone. He thought of the news reporter and picked up the phone.

"Channel Six," she answered. "Anna Allison, may I help you?" Russell hadn't expected to get straight through to the newsroom.

"This is Russell Thompson," he said. "Has there been any news on the identity of the old man found in the alley?"

"Are you with the press?" she asked.

"No, just a friend," he answered. "Someone he touched with his life."

She hesitated. "His name was Charles Cawley," Anna said. "We are trying to do a profile on him. Is there any way we could get together? Maybe you could help."

"I'd really like that," Russell said, "but there are a few things that I've got to do."

There was no way he would be telling anyone about these pictures until he had some explanation.

"Perhaps we could talk after the funeral tomorrow," Anna pushed. "Will you be there?"

"I'd like to," Russell said. "Where is it being held?"

"There's a wake at his home at 1112 Adams Street. That's on the West Side. It's at 2 o'clock. Maybe I'll see you there," she said.

No one needed or wanted to know more about Charles Cawley than Russell. At least now he would be able to put a name to his friend's face.

Russell parked down the block from the house on Adams Street. As he walked up to the house, he could see that it was not expensive, but it had been well maintained. Not what he expected at all. Why had he just assumed that the man was homeless?

He could hear the sounds of a spiritual being sung. The door was slightly ajar. He looked in. The room was filled with family and friends saying good-bye to Cawley. Russell stepped inside. Nothing about this man was predictable. His friends were eclectic both in age and color. The deacon began to speak.

"Charles Cawley was a friend of mine for sixty-two years. No, not *was* my friend, *is* my friend. A while back something remarkable happened to him. He said to me, 'Deacon, I learned something valuable today. Once you know you are in a hole, you gotta stop diggin'.' What a hole he must have been in. But true to Charles's form he found a way out. He was never happier than the last six months of his life.

"So don't feel bad for old Charles Cawley, he's just made a new beginning. Christmas is a season of new beginnings. It's a season of hope, a season of joy, and a season of rebirth.

Charles saw the future and saw a better place. He always had the gift of music in him. So, as we remember him today, let's remember him through his music."

A piano player began to play a gospel song and the room began to sing along with the deacon.

When my master reaches down,
I'll be there.
Takes me to that higher ground,
I'll be there.

I felt lonely, lost, and hollow,
He gave me roads that I could follow.
When my master reaches down
I'll be there.

When my savior takes my hand,
I'll be there.
Takes me to the promised land,
I'll be there.

When my deeds on earth I face,
Someone else will take my place.
When my master takes my hand,
I'll be there.

When my Jesus calls me home,
I'll be there,
Takes me home to Galilee,
I'll be there.

When He sent the world His Son,
He would save us every one.
When my Jesus calls me home
I'll be there.

Russell looked around the small house. It was modest but cozy. The room was filled with photographs, all in black and white. Suddenly Russell froze. On a small table he saw the

picture of Cawley and himself. It was the same black-and-white photo he had in his pocket. The service ended and the room began to clear.

An elderly woman approached Russell. He recognized her from photos in the room. It had to be Cawley's wife. "Welcome, Mr. Thompson."

Russell felt that same cold chill go through him.

"Cawley said you'd be coming." She smiled. "Looks like his work has been done. He said to study those pictures real hard. All you need to know is right there and the good you'll get from the future will keep the past from feeling so bad. He said you'd come to know what I mean."

Near the door Russell noticed the television newscaster. He walked toward her, and smiled. "Anna . . . It's nice to meet you."

"Quite a friend you had, Mr. Thompson. They all seemed to love him very much. I feel a little uncomfortable coming here, being a reporter and all. They stopped me at the door and I kind of told them I was with you. I hope that's OK?"

Russell was flattered. He wasn't sure how to respond.

After all, this was the first woman in seventeen years that he had bothered to notice whether or not she was beautiful. And she was. "With me?...That's fine," he said. "But if you're going to, you should probably call me Russell."

"OK Russell, can we go somewhere and talk about my profile on Charles Cawley?" Anna asked.

"If it's a profile you want, these are the people to ask, not me. They knew him better than I did." There were two things that Russell was sure of. He did not need to be a part of this profile, because he did not want to be "The Christmas Hero," and he certainly did not have time for the distractions Anna could create. He had been chosen for some kind of mission, and he had a feeling that time was of the essence. He gave her a quick smile and walked toward the door.

Outside, as he got into his car, he noticed that a light snow had begun to fall again. He started the car and then turned it off again. He had to stop for a moment and try to make some sense out of what Cawley's wife had told him. Cawley had told her to tell him something about "the joy of the future and the pain of the past not feeling so bad." Boy, could he use that.

Russell sat at home at his desk and examined the second photo. It was taken of him in an "L" mass-transit train car. He was kneeling over a woman, holding her in his arms. Her coat was old and worn. Wrapped around her neck was a bold checkered scarf. Her face was turned toward him so that it couldn't be seen in the picture. Outside, the station sign read "Highland Heights." Further on a neon sign proclaimed, "Only fifteen more shopping days 'til Christmas."

He checked his calendar. *That was tomorrow.* He would have to be there, but what time of day? Was it getting dark, or was the sun just coming up? There was no way to know. He had no choice but to be at the station early. He wished that he had known the time a little better, or what to expect. To be on the safe side, he'd be there at six in the morning.

Russell doubted that he could sleep with all this running through his head. As he dozed off he couldn't help thinking he was crazy. No one in his right mind ran around chasing pictures that hadn't happened yet. But the truth was, he had nothing else to do.

Russell slept well again. He got up and ground some fresh coffee. He decided that today was the day he would try to make it. Kirsten would have laughed, but she would have loved the fact that he was trying.

He went to the Highland Heights station. It was still dark. It was Saturday and the usually busy station wasn't crowded. Many of the train cars were almost empty. From which direction would it come?

He took the photo from his pocket. Everything was in its place. The Highland Heights sign was on the wall. The neon light was blinking. He was here on the right day and it was the right station. But what time of day?

He waited and watched, observing people coming and going. Few seemed to have any holiday spirit. They were just making their way. An elderly couple walked hand-in-hand. They were taking their time, enjoying their moments together. Suddenly there was a commotion in one of the arriving cars.

"She's down!" someone yelled, as everyone scattered. Russell wondered why people ran away whenever someone fell. He made his way through the crowd and jumped on the car just as the doors were closing.

"Call 911," he yelled back. "Have them meet me at the next stop!"

The train left the station. For a brief moment all the components of the picture in his hand came together. This was indeed some kind of divine intervention.

The lady lay on the floor screaming in pain. "My baby! My baby! It's time!"

"You'll be OK," Russell tried to comfort her. "They've called for help."

She grimaced in pain. It was obvious now that he had not been sent here only to comfort her. He was going to deliver her baby, here at Christmastime.

It was quite a scene as the train pulled to a stop at the next station. A medical alert team was ready. A crowd of curious onlookers had gathered. The doors to the train hissed open. On the floor Russell held the woman. In her arms a young infant wrapped in Russell's coat cried out to the new world. Just a few days ago, Russell thought, he was ready to give up his life. Now he was responsible for a new one.

The medical team took charge, helping the woman and the baby. Russell watched as they brought them to the

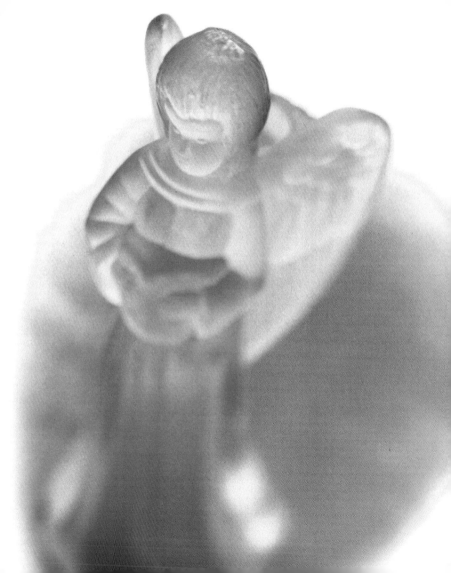

ambulance, then he slipped away into the crowd and disappeared.

L ater at home he flipped on the television and watched Anna as she reported the evening news.

"The Christmas Hero was busy again," she said. "Let's go to Tonya Evans at the scene."

"Well, Anna, our hero was at it again today. A young, pregnant homeless woman, Theresa Alverez, had been riding the train to stay out of the cold. Here at the Highland Heights station she went into labor. A silver-haired man jumped into the car and delivered the baby. This station is all abuzz about this guy. He disappeared as quickly as he had appeared. Back to you, Anna."

Anna's co-anchor quickly added, "Sounds a little like a super hero, don't you think, Anna?"

She smiled and looked into the camera, "I don't know, but I hope so. Good night, Christmas Hero, wherever you are."

Russell was exhausted and had fallen asleep, not hearing her newscast of the day's other events.

He woke up the next morning and again started the day with his fresh-brewed coffee. Outside a snowfall had blanketed the city. Like a new coat of paint over dirty old walls, the city sparkled under the early morning light. As he sat staring out the window, bits and pieces of last night's dream started coming back to him. *It was a good dream*, he thought. At least he felt good when he woke up. That was usually an indication of how his night had gone.

In his dream he and Kirsten were in a long, mirrored corridor with mirrored doors. They were laughing so hard, just trying to find the doors. Every time they went in a door it opened into some place they had been together. As Russell pieced his dream together, he realized that, door by door, it was replaying their life. Then his mind went blank. Something strange kept blocking his vision.

"Please God . . . don't let it end here." He loved all these memories with Kirsten. He closed his eyes and reached for something—anything—an image.

Little by little it came back. Now he knew why it hadn't come at first. As the next-to-the-last door opened, he came out alone. He went back in the dark, silent room time and time again, but he could never find Kirsten. He felt his chest tighten. This was supposed to be a good dream. As he exited the room for the last time, he looked back and thought he saw her. He lunged back toward the door, but he was too late and it slammed shut. He stepped back. All the doors he had passed through had vanished. The corridor was now only a mirror. There was one final door left.

As Russell opened the door, a bright flash of light struck him in the face. He covered his eyes as he went in. He saw a crowd of people . . . faceless people all smiling.

How could faceless people be smiling? he thought. But they were. It was all so surreal, but he remembered he felt good. He was glad he had continued his dream. When the phone rang, he wasn't sure if it was part of his dream. As it rang the second time he opened his eyes and realized his time with Kirsten was over.

"Hello, this is Russell."

"Hi, it's Anna. What's your day like? Any chance we could have lunch and talk about Charles Cawley?"

There was an unusually long pause in the conversation. For a second Russell had drifted back to the room full of faceless people. The sound of Anna's voice had triggered

something. He got the feeling that she had been one of them, but how?

"I'd really like to," Russell said, "but today is really hectic for me." Why was he running from her? he wondered. "I promise you in the next couple of days we'll get together."

She understood . . . and he liked that about her.

Russell got out the remaining pictures. He had work to do. As he looked for the message in the next photograph, he thought the more he looked, the less he saw. He didn't like this part, not because it was too much trouble, but because he was afraid he would miss something and not be there in time. He got out a piece of paper and wrote down the clues from the third picture:

1. Marshall Field's department store
2. Clock reads 9:18
3. Little girl
4. White bear

There were no obvious clues to the date. He continued to look. There must be something. A newspaper with headlines in the picture. He had seen that on an episode of Perry

Mason. There were none. Signs. As Russell scanned the picture he noticed a small sign. It was too small to read. He took out his reading glasses and used them like a magnifying glass. Now he could see.

"Santa arrives today at 9 A.M.," it read.

Russell jumped up. Old Cawley was right. All he needed to know was right there. Russell called information and then called Marshall Field's. "What day does Santa start at the store?" Russell asked.

"December 15th," the operator said, "but you had better get here early because there will be a line around the block."

"Thanks," he said and hung up the phone. He looked at his calendar. Today was the eleventh. He had four days. He wished now that he hadn't said no to Anna.

He hadn't heard from Anna in days. He had been tempted to call her, but that was a door he couldn't afford to open just yet. He had to get downtown.

Russell tucked the photos into his pocket and headed down to the department store. The street scene was magical. There was fresh snow, and the bustling shoppers and festive decorations were a perfect mix. There was an unusually long line outside the store. As he stood in line he looked through the window into the store. He remembered how, as a boy, his behavior was particularly good this time of year. He watched as shoppers searched for the perfect gift. *Was there such a thing?* he wondered.

Behind him a little girl nervously asked her father, "Will Momma like her gift, Daddy? What if we don't have enough money?"

Her older brother was concerned. "We've got to get to Santa, Dad. How long are we going to have to wait to get inside?"

"Momma will like a heart, won't she, Daddy?" the little girl asked.

"It can't be a very big one," her brother said, "not with our money. That's why we have to see Santa."

Russell looked at the family. The young father kept his arm around his little girl, as her coat was thin and the wind quite cold. His little boy's tennis shoes were worn.

The line inched forward. As he moved closer to the door Russell saw the Channel 6 News van pull up in front of the store. They had followed him, he thought, annoyed. Anna stepped out of the van. Russell was upset. He left his place in line and approached the van.

The little girl called after him, "Hey mister, should we save your place?"

He didn't answer. Instead he spoke to Anna. "So you had to follow me. You just couldn't leave me alone. You had to have your story. I should have known."

Suddenly bells started ringing and people were cheering. "I've got to go," Anna said, brushing past him.

Russell looked over to the ringing bells. The store manager took a microphone and began to speak. "Shoppers, we have our 25,000th customer! Here they are, the Ryan family!" The family that had been standing behind Russell stepped up to the microphone. Their smiles lit up the street.

The manager continued, "As our 25,000th customer, you have won a $5,000 shopping spree! What are you going to get?" He put the mike to the little girl.

"Something for my momma," she said proudly.

The news crew was capturing it all as Anna looked on.

Russell came up to her. "Look, I'm sorry," he tried to apologize. "It's just that things are happening so fast, and I'm not sure what's next. You're a news person. Maybe you could help me." He was cut off by the young boy who came up and grabbed his hand.

"Hey, mister, come with us! My dad said that if you hadn't gotten out of line we wouldn't have won."

Anna gave Russell a look of disbelief. The boy began to drag him back toward the store.

"Will you meet me later?" Russell asked Anna.

"Call me at the station," she said.

The manager led them to the toy department first. "Mister, can you reach up and get me the white teddy bear, please?"

Russell reached up for the bear, just as he had in the photo, and handed it to the little girl.

He spent the afternoon with the Ryan family as they shopped through the store. The laughter of the young

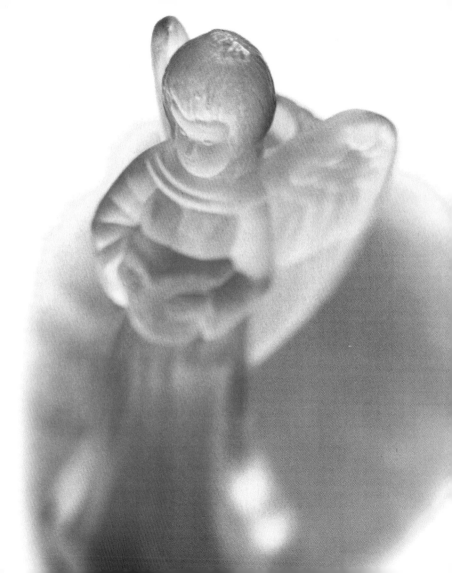

children began to reach the child inside him. They finished their shopping and said their good-byes outside the store. Russell turned to go.

"Wait a minute!" the little girl shouted. She ran up and gave him a hug. "Merry Christmas," she said.

"Merry Christmas," Russell said, and he meant it.

As he walked from the store into the streets, he noticed that Christmas had officially come to Chicago. It was almost like a movie set. He had never seen so many lights before. *Is the city this beautiful every year?* he wondered. As he passed an exclusive women's store he noticed something—a beautiful outfit. *That would look great on Anna . . . I mean Kirsten. Why would I have thought that? I did mean Kirsten,* he thought.

It had been almost ten days since he had watched the film of Kirsten. Had he become selfish now that his life was filling up again? Was he forgetting her? He flipped on the television. He paused before he hit the play button. He dreaded the next few moments. It would be either pain or guilt. Neither would be pleasant.

He sat in the dark room with only the light of the TV. He closed his eyes and said a silent prayer. "God, you've given me a lot to deal with in the last year. I can only hope you have a plan. I feel lost right now . . . could use some help." Russell realized that he hadn't actually prayed since Kirsten's death. But it didn't hurt to ask.

He reached over and hit the play button on the VCR. He had forgotten to rewind the tape. The first image was a freeze-frame of Kirsten waving and smiling at him. He didn't remember what would come next. The tape continued. She blew him a kiss and said, "I love you, I've gotta go now," and she ran off down the beach out of sight. He felt the tears run down his cheeks.

"Me too, Kirsten. I will always love you . . . but I guess I have to go now too." As he turned off the VCR, the Channel 6 News popped on the screen. It was Anna interviewing the Ryan family. This could not be a coincidence.

It had been over a week since Russell had heard from Anna. He had, however, watched her every night on the news. He had watched her for several years, but had never noticed her smile until now. *It's funny,* he thought, *how people look so different once you meet them in person.*

He was more than a bit embarrassed by what had happened outside Marshall Field's, but he had always been a private person, and the thought of him being a public hero scared him to death.

Russell had spent the last week studying the final photo and sorting out his personal and financial life. Things had gotten so much better for him that sometimes it was hard to believe. He had been offered a job at the hospital where Kirsten had been doing public relations. He had written them a letter of appreciation last week in which he had used Cawley's statement, "Where there is future, there is hope." It was the perfect slogan for their new cancer wing. The job was perfect for him.

He picked up the phone and called Anna and asked to meet her.

"I've got to put a story together," she said, "and I need to stop by and check on someone, but that should just take a few minutes."

"So why don't I pick you up?" Russell asked. "I'll take you

to wherever you need to go and then we can get a bite to eat."

"Sounds good to me," she said. "Pick me up around five."

He pulled out the final photograph. In it he was standing in front of what looked like a hospital bed. The room was sparsely furnished. The way that he stood, he couldn't see who was in the bed. A black-striped raincoat hung over the back of a chair next to the bed. He hadn't really studied the picture that much before. There had been no need to. But now was the time. He took out his pen and paper to write down the clues but this time there were none. Just him, a bed with someone in it, and a chair with a striped raincoat on it. Nothing else. No newspapers, no clocks, no neon signs, nothing.

Cawley had promised him everything he needed would be there. He closed his eyes and looked up. "God, I may need your help on this one. Get me there somehow. This is my last picture. I don't want to fail, but I just don't know what to do."

How his life had changed. It had all started with the gift of a topcoat and camera. But it wasn't just his life that had changed, he had changed. He realized how aware he had become, how he had taken time to notice the elderly couple at the station laughing and enjoying every moment. Then there was the new fallen snow and the laughter in the eyes of the children. The ability to see all this had been trapped inside of him since Kirsten's death. But he was beginning to awaken.

Russell pulled his car up in front of the television station. An earlier snowfall had now turned to a light rain and his windshield wipers smeared the front window. He saw her running out the front door of the station. A bolt of fear ran through his body. Anna was wearing a black-striped rain coat. As she made her way to the car he looked at the photo one more time. He studied it closely. There was no doubt in his mind that it was her coat in the picture. That was her in the bed. He would stay with her until whatever was supposed to happen, happened. Then he would be by her side to help her.

As Anna stepped into the car she said, "So, I'm actually being picked up and having dinner with the 'Christmas Hero,'" she said happily. "I just have to make one stop."

"Remember, I am no hero," Russell said nervously. The rain began to freeze on the windshield and Russell could barely see. Only good things had been happening, but now he felt an old enemy—fear.

The windshield wipers swished at a hypnotic pace, back and forth . . . back and forth. Russell had never driven so carefully in his life. He could imagine a lot of ways that she could end up in that bed and he sure didn't want it to be his fault. He swerved to miss an oncoming car that wasn't even close to him.

"Are you all right?" she asked.

He realized he hadn't heard a word she had been saying since she got into the car.

"I need to stop at 815 South Eighth just for a minute," Anna said. "Then I want you to tell me about your magic power."

"It's not a very safe side of town," he said. "Are you sure you need to go down there tonight?"

"I'm a reporter, remember?" she reminded him. "I go to all parts of town."

"Just be careful," he warned. "It looks pretty slippery

out there."

The windows began to fog up, so he cracked his window to let in some air. *Be careful*, he thought, *be careful*. He couldn't let anything happen, not now.

A car pulled up next to him filled with a local gang. He rolled up his window. *Be careful*. This was the neighborhood where he had been walking only a few weeks before. He turned off on Eighth Street as the car next to him kept on going straight. He pulled up in front of the house. A couple of streetlights were out. The wind whipped up and Anna clutched her coat.

"Why don't you wait here?" Anna said. "This should only take a minute."

There was no way Russell was going to let her go in the house alone. "Maybe I should come with you. This looks like kind of a tough neighborhood."

"You're right about that," she said. "Don't leave anything in the car."

Russell grabbed his briefcase and the camera from the back seat and walked her to the door.

A young Mexican woman answered their knock. "He's

asleep," she said, "but come on in."

Anna turned to Russell, "I'll be just a moment." She walked into a back bedroom.

Russell paced in the front hallway. It was hard not to look at the photos hanging on the wall. Russell felt a bit like he was intruding in this family's life. There were twenty to thirty pictures. They seemed to be in some sort of chronological order. There was a mother in the hospital with two identical sons with the father, who was wearing gang colors. Then there were five or six pictures of the boys at various ages. At what looked to be nine or ten years old they had already taken on the look of "The Hood." They were bangers. There were other pictures of the boys in their teens with their girlfriends. They were, in fact, a very handsome family.

Then the pictures changed. They became newspaper clippings. One headline read, "Local Boy Promises Slain Brother 'I Will Clean Up Gangs In Your Memory'." Below the headline was a picture of Ramone Dominguez and Channel 6 reporter Anna Allison. On the table beneath the photos lay a newspaper dated December 8. In bold letters the headline read, "Local Hero Gunned Down By Gang Members He Vowed To Change." In the picture the mayor stood next to Ramone's bed and presented him with the key to the city. He declared Ramone "Everybody's Hero." *December 8*, Russell thought, *that must be the kid who was gunned down the night I met Cawley.*

From the other room came a scream, *"Oh, my God!"* and a large crash.

Russell burst through the door, not knowing what to expect. His heart was pounding. He knew he shouldn't have let her out of his sight. There on the floor was a large mirror that had fallen near Anna. Ramone's mother was on her knees next to her, making sure she wasn't injured. As he looked around the room, it hit him like a bolt of lightning. In the picture it was Ramone in the bed. The sense of relief he felt was overwhelming. *God does work in mysterious ways*, he thought.

Russell looked at Anna. She was fine, but it looked as if she had been crying. He walked to Ramone's bedside and, as was the case every time he reached the moment of the photograph, a shiver went up his spine. Ramone had slept

through it all.

Russell looked back at Anna. Her tears were not as much for herself as for Ramone. She was the one who had put him on the front page and drawn all the attention to him. She was worried about him and felt responsible. If not for her, he might have been able to achieve his dream.

Anna approached Russell's side. She took Ramone's hand and said, "What you are doing is important to all of us." She was sure he must have heard her because she thought she felt him squeeze her hand.

As they left the room, Russell took one look back at the Brownie Hawkeye camera that he had left on the table beside Ramone's bed. *He is young,* he thought, *and where there is future, there is hope.* Ramone Dominguez could use the camera, and the world could use more Ramone Dominguezes.

On Christmas morning Russell woke early. He fixed his pot of coffee and reflected on how close he had come to wasting his life, and how rich it seemed now. Why hadn't he asked her last night to spend Christmas Day with him? he thought.

He tried to call her.

"Hi, this is Anna, I'm working today, call me at the office. Thanks."

His heart sank. It shouldn't be like this, not on Christmas. Maybe she was working because she had nothing else to do. Russell quickly dialed her office.

"Channel 6 News. Can I help you?"

It wasn't her.

"Can I speak to Anna?" Russell asked.

"She's out on assignment," the voice stated.

"Ask her to call Russell when she returns, please."

"I sure will," the voice replied, then a dial tone. Needless to say, this was not what he had hoped for on this Christmas Day. As he settled into his favorite chair, he took a moment to count his blessings.

Russell could never in a million years have prepared himself for what he saw when he answered the doorbell that Christmas Day. There stood Anna, Cawley's wife, Theresa and her baby, the Ryan family, and an entire Channel 6 News crew. These were the faceless smiling people from his dream and their photos would take their place on the mantle alongside his most-valued pictures of Kirsten. They had become Russell's family, and they brought with them a Christmas tree, presents, food, and the most precious gift of all—laughter. As they sat down for their Christmas meal the words from a seasonal song came from the radio.

> Let's all gather around at the table
> In the spirit of family and friends.
> And we'll all join hands and remember this moment
> 'Til the season comes 'round again.

Christmas had come to Russell Allen Thompson.